Bright Summaries.com

Soft song

by Leïla Slimani

Soft song

by Leïla Slimani

LEÏLA SLIMANI

FRENCH-MOROCCAN JOURNALIST AND NOVELIST

- **Born in 1981 in Rabat (Morocco)**
- **Some of his works**:
  - *In the Ogre's Garden* (2014), novel
  - *Sex and Lies* (2017), essay

Leïla Slimani comes from a French-speaking Moroccan family and belongs to an affluent background. Her father is a senior Moroccan civil servant who studied in France. Her mother, a French-Moroccan, is a doctor. With her baccalaureate obtained at the French Lycée in Rabat, she went to Paris and the Lycée Fénelon to begin a literary preparatory class. After graduating from the Institute of Political Studies in Paris and trying her hand at acting, she trained as a journalist at *L'Express* before being hired at the newspaper *Jeune Afrique* in 2008. In 2012, she decided to devote herself to literary writing. In 2014, she published her first novel, *Dans le jardin de l'ogre* (*In the Garden of the Ogre), which* received critical acclaim. Her second novel, *Chanson douce*, won the Goncourt Prize in 2016. A year later, Leïla SLimani published an essay, *Sexe et mensonge*, devoted to "sexual misery in the Maghreb". She says she is influenced by Chekhov, who "loves his characters" and "never judges them", as well as by Stefan Zweig and Milan Kundera.

SOFT SONG

A NOVEL BASED ON A NEWS STORY

- **Genre**: novel

- **Reference edition**: SLIMANI L., *Chanson douce*, Paris, Éditions Gallimard, 2016, 227 p.

- **1st edition**: 2016

- **Themes**: crime, family, education, addiction, contemporary society, professional success, money, social classes

Mila and Adam, the children of Myriam and Paul Massé, are found brutally murdered. The person responsible for this atrocious crime is Louise, their nanny, who was hired by the Parisian couple when Myriam decided to go back to work as a lawyer. The narrator goes back in time, according to the principle of analepsis, to try to understand the reasons for this tragedy. At first, everything suggests that Louise is the ideal nanny, perfectly assisting Myriam and Paul at home. But as time goes by, Louise's presence becomes unnaturally intrusive, as if she wanted to become a full member of the family. Her dependence grows and becomes increasingly unbearable. With a sharp and incisive style, taking the form of terse and raw statements, and with a lively rhythm marked by short chapters, Leïla Slimani tackles contemporary issues such as the family, the education of children, professional success, and class prejudices. It also reflects on the relationships of dependence and power between individuals. For this novel, the author was inspired by a news item that occurred in the United States on 25 October 2012: a mother of three children finds two of her children stabbed to death in her Upper West Side flat. The perpetrator is their nanny: she slit her own throat but did not die.

SUMMARY

When Myriam Massé returned from work early, she found her two children stabbed. Adam is dead on the spot, Mila succumbs to her wounds on the way to the hospital. The criminal is their nanny. Still at the scene, she tried to commit suicide but failed. She is in a coma.

About a year and a half earlier, the Massé couple started looking for a nanny following Myriam's decision to start a career as a lawyer. Pregnant with Mila at the end of her studies, she devoted herself to her daughter and later to her son, leaving her professional career on the back burner. Today, she can no longer stand staying at home and is finding it increasingly difficult to be a stay-at-home mother. Paul works a lot on his own as a producer. They need someone they can trust to look after the children during the day. After a few fruitless searches, Louise was recommended to them. The couple chose her without hesitation as if it were a matter of course.

Louise is perfect, a real fairy. She conscientiously takes care of the children, but also of the house: she tidies up, sorts, and prepares the dinner. She even goes so far as to change the decoration of the living room. Myriam and Paul are seduced and amused. Because Myriam can devote herself to her work without being hindered by domestic constraints she finds hiring Louise a right step in the right direction. Louise becomes indispensable, arriving earlier and earlier and leaving later and later. The children no longer ask for their parents. Myriam appreciates Louise's invisible and efficient presence and even gives her gifts. It is the nanny who cooks when Paul and Myriam receive friends.

On a whim, Paul offers to take Louise on a holiday to a Greek island. The nanny is seduced by the softness of the place, the light breeze, the sun, the warmth. She appreciates the lightness of the evenings in the restaurant. The only problem is that she cannot swim. She pushes Mila away, to everyone's surprise, when she wants to force her to swim. So Paul teaches her to swim. She likes the feel of the water on her body. She feels good. When the trip ends, the return to her flat in Créteil at the weekend leaves her distraught and morose. Fortunately, the warmth of September still allows for picnics and trips to the park.

However, winter sets in and brings with it the first incident: Louise has made Mila up excessively, for fun. Paul is offended, reprimands her and almost stops all contact with her. Vexed, Louise feels alone and panics. It is then Myriam's turn to discover two scars on Adam's shoulder. When questioned, Louise accuses the toddler's sister, saying she was bitten herself. In reality, if Mila had bitten her, it was because Louise had held the little girl's chest very tightly against her, scolding her for having wandered off too far during a walk in the park. The family's departure for the mountains for a week increases Louise's unease. She feels abandoned and stays at home. She declares to Wafa, a nanny she met in the square, that she would like to stay permanently on the island of Sifnos during their next family trip to Greece. One day, Paul and Myriam receive a letter from the Treasury, urging them to deduct from Louise's salary the amount she has owed to the State for several months. Affected by the couple's reproaches, the nanny has two anxious nights. Indeed, Louise is feeling worse and worse. Faced with her distress, Myriam blames herself. However, the distance between the two women kept escalating. One evening, Myriam finds a chicken carcass sitting in the middle of the kitchen table. Deeply disturbed, unaware of the significance of this scene, she vaguely senses a danger in Louise's person.

Springtime gives Louise a little optimism. Without enthusiasm, she starts seeing Hervé, whom Wafa has introduced to her. Then she begins to dream of a baby that Myriam and Paul could conceive. Determined to make this project a success, she takes the children to a restaurant to leave their parents alone. However, a final incident destroys her optimism: her landlord gives her notice to leave the flat because of unpaid rent. From then on, she sinks into a deep melancholy. She has great difficulty tolerating the children and is irritated by their cries and questions. She leaves the television on all day. The last time the family saw Louise before the crime was in the car on their way home from a day out with friends.

In the last chapter, the narrator returns to the arrival of Captain Nina Dorval at the scene of the crime, to the testimonies of Wafa and the neighbour, and to what

Paul reports about the murder weapon. Two months of investigation have passed. It is the end of August. Nina is about to reconstruct the crime scene. She will play the role of Louise.

CHARACTER STUDY

LOUISE

Louise is the nanny hired by Paul and Myriam Massé. With her slim figure, she looks twenty years old, although she is more like forty. Blonde, her face riddled with tiny freckles; she exudes something childlike. She invariably wears a long skirt, a blouse and patent ballerinas. Her bun above the neck gives her a strict look. Her nails are manicured and her eyes are made up. Louise "is not unpleasant to look at", according to Paul.

Her husband is dead. She has a daughter, Stephanie, aged twenty, who ran away and never came back. Louise lives in a one-room flat, which she tidies up very carefully. She has had several employers, including M. Franck and the Rouviers, who speak highly of her to the Massés.

Louise is dedicated, a perfectionist and carries out all the tasks she is given with the utmost meticulousness, almost maniacal. There is something old-fashioned about her manner. When they met her for the first time, Paul and Myriam didn't hesitate for a second: she's the one for the job, it's obvious. Moreover, Louise showed great confidence with the children the first time she met them. The children adopted her immediately. She is a great housekeeper. She is also a good cook.

This nanny is very maternal with Adam and manages to tame Mila, who is more shy. She knows how to have fun with children and takes all entertainment seriously. She particularly enjoys playing hide-and-seek and likes to tell "cruel tales where the good guys die in the end" (p39). Capable of tenderness, she can also have unexplained violent reactions. A good example is the day in the park when she holds Mila too tightly to her because she has wandered off without warning. It soon becomes clear that she has a complex relationship with the little girl. Since the incident in the park, each has a grievance against the other.

It is known that Louise has had an episode of 'delusional melancholy' in the past, for which she was hospitalised. She still sometimes falls into a morbid state when her relations with the Massés deteriorate.

Louise keeps her distance from adults, except with Myriam, to whom she is close at first. However, a distance is gradually established between the two women. Paul, touched by her fragility, teaches her to swim in Greece and Louise appreciates his presence. But he no longer speaks to her when he discovers that she has made up Mila excessively. Louise becomes friends with Wafa, another Muslim nanny who has recently arrived in France and whom she met in the square. She has a brief relationship with Hervé, a man she does not like.

MYRIAM

Myriam has put her career as a lawyer on hold to raise her two children. By the time the story begins, she is frustrated with her life as a stay-at-home mother, and decides to start working again and hire a nanny. She resents her husband for not taking her wishes for emancipation seriously enough. A chance meeting with Pascal, an old school friend, is the trigger. He offers her a job as a lawyer in his office. Myriam is very conscientious and works tirelessly from morning to night, sometimes even at night. She is friends with Emma, a woman who is happy in her role as a model housewife. She feels mothered by Louise and appreciates being able to rely on her to look after the children and maintain the house. Both of them have the habit of having tea together in the kitchen. Indeed, Myriam enjoys Louise's company and regularly gives her gifts. However, with each successive misunderstanding, their relationship begins to crack.

Myriam has a stormy relationship with her mother-in-law. She has been angry with her since a memorable discussion during which Sylvie reproached her daughter-in-law for thinking only of her personal ambition, and for not being available for her children, making her responsible for their capricious nature.

It is Myriam who discovers her murdered children.

PAUL

He is Myriam's husband. He accepts her decision to start working, even if he makes a mockery of her ambitions. A music producer, he devotes a lot of time to his work and is pleased that his business is growing, having had to put aside his professional aspirations temporarily when he became a father, to the point of losing confidence in his abilities. His mother, Sylvie, who has brought him up with a left-wing ideology and feels that he has denied his origins and has become more middle-class, has a great influence on him. Paul is satisfied with Louise's presence. One day, he even offers her to stay for dinner with their friends, before announcing that she will go on holiday with them. He teaches her to swim. However, their relationship deteriorates definitively when one evening he finds his daughter Mila wearing outrageous make-up from the nanny.

THE CHILDREN

Mila

Mila is a fierce child. She is temperamental and can throw herself on the ground in the middle of the street. She is obsessed with her image and looks at herself a lot in shop windows. She is frail and graceful.

She is 'clever' with Louise (p. 39). She is disobedient and manipulative in order to make the nanny give in to her wishes. However, she also has moments of guilt when she is more loving. She enjoys the cruel tales her nanny tells her. Little by little, she allows herself to be tamed by Louise. However, their relationship is very conflictual and sometimes involves physical power struggles. When Louise held her too tightly to punish her for wandering off alone in the park, Mila bit her. When Mila forced her to go swimming in Greece despite her repeated refusals, Louise pushed her away too forcefully. One evening, Louise took the children to a restaurant and forced them to take long diversions through Paris. Exhausted, Mila is torn between incomprehension and anguish. On the day of the crime, she dies in the ambulance taking her to the hospital.

Adam

He was still a baby when Louise was engaged. Yet he shows tenderness to this motherly woman. Moreover, he seems to take Louise's side when her father reprimands her for putting makeup on Mila. It is his voice that closes the story when he asks his mother where Louise is going, whom they see on the pavement. Adam is hit by Louise and dies instantly.

SECONDARY CHARACTERS

Stéphanie

She is Louise's daughter. She is twenty years old. As a child, she followed her mother to her various employers, never feeling like she belonged. She felt like a nuisance. As a teenager, she put Louise to the test: she regularly snuck out of the house, spent her nights out and abandoned her schooling. One day, she ended up not coming back, 'as if she was obviously destined to' (p. 90). Louise later learns that she is in the South and has fallen in love.

Jacques

He is Louise's late husband. Very contemptuous of his wife, angry and wasteful; he left her nothing but debts.

After his death, she had only one month to leave their house, which was about to be seized.

Wafa

She is the nanny Louise met in the square. Very talkative, and no more than twenty-five years old. Undocumented, she arrived in France through a prostitution network. She now looks after a little boy. With her curves, her unkempt appearance and the way she holds herself, Louise finds her a bit vulgar. She bakes fat pastries and offers them to her regularly. She tells her about her life, invites her to her wedding and is devastated when she learns of her friend's crime.

Sylvie

She is Paul's mother. She disapproves of her son and daughter-in-law's lifestyle, their professional ambitions and their hierarchical relationship with Louise. A left-wing activist; she has instilled in her son values that she accuses him of denying. She is particularly virulent towards Myriam, going so far as to make her feel guilty for not looking after her children all day.

Hervé

He is a man that Wafa introduced to Louise at her wedding. He has done some work on her house. Louise feels nothing but disgust for Hervé: he is banal, small, has a head on his shoulders and his hands are those of a worker. She nevertheless agrees to go out with him and gives in to his advances without enthusiasm.

Rose Grinberg

She is the Massés' neighbour. She is sixty-five years old and a former music teacher. She blames herself for noticing Louise's strange behaviour an hour before the crime without raising the alarm, just as she regrets not having paid more attention to Louise's confidences about her money problems. She was napping during the crime. She heard Myriam's screams when she opened the shutters.

Hector Rouvier

He was looked after by Louise as a child. He is eighteen years old when he learns of his former nanny's crime and is questioned by the police. He remembers Louise's hands on his childish body, her caresses, her smell and 'the sudden savagery of her love' (p. 166). He realises that he has always known that he was under threat.

Mr. Franck

He employed Louise when she was twenty-five. He was a painter and lived with her mother, whom Louise looked after. He demands that she have an abortion when he learns that she is pregnant. Louise did not resist but did not wake up on time on the day of the operation. As a result, she never returns to his home.

KEYS TO READING

CHRONICLE OF A DRAMA FORETOLD

The genre of the chronicle corresponds to an account of events that follows the order in which they took place. *Chanson douce* is similar to a chronicle from this point of view. It is special in that it chronologises events whose outcome is known from the start. The narrative is therefore an analepse.

The advent of crime

Indeed, the novel opens directly with the description of the crime scene. The murder of the Massé family's children by their nanny has already taken place and is known to the reader. This shows that the narrator does not wish to create suspense that she does not launch into a story that would lead to a final revelation. What interests her is rather to shed light on the causes, to go back over the events that may have led to such a tragedy. For this reason, the last chapter returns to the temporality of the prologue by focusing on the discovery of the double murder and the reconstruction of the crime scene by Captain Nina Dorval. Leïla Slimani chooses to follow the course of events and the evolution of Louise's character. The second chapter opens with Myriam's search for a nanny. Then, as the pages go by, the narrator recounts her behaviour as a perfect nanny, her attention to the children and parents, her immersion and then intrusion into the Massé family, the trips she takes with them, her obsessive desire for closeness, the first tensions, the rise of Louise's delirious melancholy, the obligation to leave her flat.

Successive illuminations

Within this chronicle, the narrator intersperses a few chapters that are flashbacks to Louise's life. The first, entitled "Stéphanie" (p. 53), named after Louise's daughter, focuses on their relationship. The second is devoted to the character of Rose Grinberg, the Massé's neighbour, who is plagued by guilt for not having reacted, for not having raised the alarm when she was surprised by Louise's behaviour in the lift a few minutes before the tragedy. She could, she says, have 'changed the course of events' (p. 82). We learn that she had already been embarrassed a month before the tragedy by an equivocal discussion with Louise. Later in the story, there is a chapter devoted to Louise's husband Jacques. In it, the author reports on his antics, his contempt for her, his reckless spending, and the debts he left her. Finally, we learn that after Jacques' death, Louise sank into delirious solitude. The story also indicates that Louise did not want to become a mother. Her first employer, Mr. Franck, learned that she was pregnant and threatened to fire her if she did not have an abortion. Without consulting her, he made an appointment with a gynaecologist for the operation. But Louise did not wake up on time on the day of her medical appointment. So she had kept her child, which she did not want and which had sprouted inside her 'like a mushroom on damp wood' (p. 111). The chapter on Hector Rouvier, a child Louise had kept ten years earlier, is not anecdotal. On the contrary, Hector's perspective on Louise is valuable: the young man reveals that 'he had always known that a threat had been hanging over him' (p. 170). Paradoxically, this flashback is part of the chronicle since it suggests the emergence of the threat, 'a white, sulphurous, unspeakable threat' (p. 170).

The last moments

Louise's growing madness is described day by day. There are three days of 'perverse lethargy' during which 'her ideas become confused' (p. 158). The text evokes Myriam's deep doubts; her growing worries as the nanny's strange behaviour multiplied. The night after the incident of the chicken carcass left by the nanny on the kitchen table, she is panicked. She thinks that Louise may be "dangerous" (p. 172), violent and may have an "appetite for revenge" (p. 172) against them. Then the pace of the narrative slows down and expands. The verbs in the present tense multiply, and the notes become increasingly detailed and circumstantial. For example, the narrator lingers on the story of Louise's outing to the restaurant with the children and tells of her feverishness: "Louise looks at the window, at her watch, at the street, at the counter on which the owner leans. She bites her nails, smiles, then her gaze becomes vague, absent" (p. 205). In the final chapters, the actions tighten up, reflecting the oppression felt by Louise: "Louise does not turn around. She continues to stare at the screen, her body completely motionless. The nanny refuses to go to the square. She doesn't want to meet the other girls or bump into the old neighbour, in front of whom she has humiliated herself by offering her services' (p. 212). This is not surprising: the story approaches the chronicle when the dramatic outcome becomes clear. The passages written from Louise's internal point of view become more important, right up to her last thought: 'I'll be punished for this, she hears herself think. I will be punished for not knowing how to love" (p. 213). All that remains is for the author to make her character disappear: that is the outcome of her chronicle. She chooses to do so symbolically, in the street, while she is being watched by the whole Massé family. "Lunar", it seems that she is waiting for something, "on the edge of a border she is about to cross and behind which she will disappear" (p. 218).

A MUTED THREAT

Chanson douce can be read as the story of an approaching threat. At first latent, hardly perceptible by Myriam and Paul, it is obvious to the warned reader. From this point of view, the novel follows a logical narrative: the structure of the novel highlights the gradual intensification of this threat and the descent into hell of the character.

A mutual love at first sight

When she talks about it, Myriam compares the first meeting with Louise to "love at first sight" (p. 28). Louise soon proves to be indispensable: she looks after the children, tidies the house, prepares the meal and only leaves once all these tasks have been completed. As if to respond to Paul's injunction, "Make yourself at home" (p. 33), she is omnipresent. She quickly becomes "invisible and indispensable" (p. 59) and becomes a full-fledged member of the family, sometimes even spending nights on the sofa. Without consulting Paul and Myriam, she transforms the living room by changing its decoration. Moreover, the narrator indicates that Louise 'patiently builds her nest in the middle of the flat' and compares her to Vishnu, 'a nurturing, jealous and protective deity' (p. 59). Myriam, for her part, accepts being mothered by this woman she knows so little about.

Worrying signs

However, her help gradually becomes intrusive. Convinced that she has an important mission to fulfil, Louise pushes Paul and Myriam to go out as often as possible. She tidies up their personal belongings and searches their privacy. She literally crashes into their lives. The story shows how she ends up sinking into identity confusion, to the point of dreaming of a third child that she could take care of, now that Mila and Adam are growing up, a child that would tie her more closely to Myriam and Paul. She desires him fanatically, like a "possessed woman" (p. 203). Moreover, during a family trip to a Greek island, Louise enjoys Paul and Myriam's mild drunkenness one night, hoping that a fruitful embrace will follow. Voyeurism is not far off, especially when she comes to watch Myriam's menstruation back in Paris. Now totally alienated, Louise wants to "make a world with them", to make a "burrow" for herself (p. 190).

Gradually, the narrator shows the first signs of disturbing behaviour through several details: Louise tells Mila and Adam cruel tales "where the good guys die in the end" (p. 39), an initial game of hide-and-seek takes a terrifying turn when Louise allows an infinite amount of time to pass before coming out of her hiding place, causing the children to panic. In response to Mila's resistance or disobedience, the nanny is brutal on two occasions: sometimes she holds her too tightly to scold her for going away without permission, and sometimes she pushes her away too forcefully when the little girl wants to force her to bathe even though she cannot swim. Finally, the chicken carcass that she ostensibly leaves on the kitchen table one evening, in such a state that 'it looks like a vulture has eaten it' (p. 163), is a macabre spectacle that is retrospectively prescient.

An empty existence

One of the strengths of the novel is that the narrator provides insights into Louise's life and personal history in a parallel and interwoven narrative. Indeed, her departures after work are mysterious to the family, as are her rare absences. She seems to fade away as if she has no other existence apart from the one she has with Paul and Myriam. It is through this parallel narrative that we learn that she lives miserably in a studio in Créteil: her husband died and left her many debts as an inheritance; her daughter, Stéphanie, left her without looking back. She never liked this woman, whom she found too submissive and who did not understand her suffering: that of a child who did not feel she belonged in the houses where her mother worked. Faced with this sad and miserable existence, faced with this solitude, it is understandable that the Massé family became a substitute family for Louise.

Louise's 'delirious melancholy

Because some of her mistakes are noticed and she is reprimanded by Myriam and Paul, Louise ends up sinking into a 'delirious melancholy' (p. 158), already identified during a past hospitalization. She feels 'like a wounded lover' (p. 177). Her melancholy and neurosis grow to the point where she can no longer go to work for the Massé family. Later, Louise feels like a hunted animal when they discover her debts, which she has never told them about. She is cornered and falls into a state of suffering, and the threat she poses becomes more and more apparent.

As the pages go by, the evolution of Louise's character increasingly chills the reader who, warned from the first chapter, sees the tragic outcome approaching. The descent into hell of this woman has begun. She is now at a dead end, an inextricable situation; that is to say, a tragic one. Neither completely good nor completely evil; she chooses horror. Myriam and Paul are unable to separate themselves from her: the nanny is so deeply rooted in their lives that she becomes impossible to dislodge. The narrator hints at Myriam's thoughts: if they push her away, Louise "will come home anyway" (p. 177). At home, she laughs less and less, she no longer goes out to the square, and the children irritate her. She leaves the television on, forcing frightening images on them. She feels the urge to strangle herself when she is near Adam. So, convinced to the end that she is acting for the good of all, as in those cruel tales she used to tell to children, Louise sinks into the most atrocious part of the human soul and gives her life.

A LOOK AT THE CONTEMPORARY WORLD

It seems that Leïla Slimani, through this story, points the finger at the shortcomings of our society, our relationship with time and the importance given to personal ambitions. The story is about the relationship between children and adults, about the place of each of them. The characters of Myriam and Paul embody these issues.

Professional ambition

Annoyed by her children and the constraints of being a housewife and jealous of her husband's professional success, Myriam becomes bitter and decides to resume her professional career. Very quickly, she works a lot, too much according to Paul. Arriving at the office at eight in the morning, before everyone else, she finishes late and is even called in at night to assist in police custody. For his part, Paul is pleased that his career is turning out the way he had hoped. According to Sylvie, Paul's mother, the children's repeated illnesses are due to Myriam's absences. Moreover, according to her, they think they are the bosses evnthough they are employees. Mila's teacher also condemns Myriam's lack of availability. How can we not hear criticism of our society? In the teacher's words: "It's the evil of the century. All these poor children are left to themselves, while both parents are consumed by the same ambition. It's simple, they're always running around. (p. 42) Indeed, Miriam and Paul are overwhelmed. There is no room for sleep or for the children. All they do is run, they 'become the bosses of a running business' (p. 118).

The illusion of the ideal family

Emma, Myriam's friend, is the embodiment of the staging of oneself and one's own that characterises our society. Her children are blond, perfect, and have 'unpronounceable names from Norse mythology' (p. 45). They are enrolled in a school that will allow them to develop their budding gifts. Emma posts "sepia-toned portraits" of her children on social networks. She is beautiful, even though she hides her anorexia by pretending to be a vegetarian. Her husband does not appear in the photos, "busy photographing this ideal family to which he belongs only as a spectator" (p. 45).

Self-fulfilment and its contradictions

Myriam is ashamed to think, without telling her friend Emma of course, that happiness will come when you no longer need others and can live your own life. Self-fulfilment, according to her, means complete freedom, without the constraints of others. Is this selfishness? The narrating voice does not comment, does not give an answer, but leaves the reader to think. Moreover, Mila's birthday party, which Louise organises with such energy and commitment, makes Myriam anxious. She is not interested in playing with the children and prefers to isolate herself in her room. However, Myriam is paradoxical, because she complains at the same time to her mother-in-law that she does not see her children, and that she suffers from this "frantic existence" (p. 131). The latter does not mince her words, accusing her daughter-in-law of selfishness and irresponsibility, claiming that she is 'at fault' for the negative development of her children, who have become capricious and tyrannical (p. 131). Myriam's contradictions are exacerbated: despite her claimed desire for freedom, she feels victimised by these accusations, as she believes many other women do. For this reason, she feels it is her duty as a mother to take photographs of her children in order to 'hold the evidence of past happiness' (p. 215) and to be able to nourish memories later on. A remark by the narrator, as if to question Myriam's determination, adds that 'it is behind the screen of her iPhone that she looks at her children' (p. 215).

A generational issue

Sylvie's convictions are used in the story to develop the thesis of a generational and ideological split. She does not understand her son's and daughter-in-law's aspirations for professional success. She invokes the values of another era, her ideals, her political commitments, and her desire for revolution. She is the voice that condemns the society of 'sell-outs' that has taken over, the one that defends a world where we would have time to live. She is not immune to contradictions either: she has worked throughout Paul's childhood, even with pride.

A social discourse

Myriam and Paul live in a beautiful building in the rue d'Hauteville, in the 10th arrondissement. They employ a woman who lives in poverty in a studio in Créteil. Emma, Myriam's friend, lives in a formerly working-class arrondissement, now occupied by a new bourgeoisie. Her comments to Louise about public schools reveal her contempt for the working classes. She intends to enrol her children in schools where their peers will belong to the same social milieu as theirs. In this respect, it is not absurd to see in *Chanson douce*, traces of a discourse on class prejudice. In the tradition of Jean Genet's Les *Bonnes*: in this play, two employees attempt to murder their boss. One might also think of Claude Chabrol's film *La Cérémonie*, which tells of the murder of an entire bourgeois family by their domestic worker with the help of the village postwoman. However, in *Chanson douce*, the crime is not socially motivated. Louise does not, like these women, have a desire for revenge. But it is clear that her financial and emotional misery, her life experience and her status as a permanent victim have generated frustrations that may have played a role in her final act. Finally, the story focuses on Wafa, a young undocumented Muslim woman who recently arrived in France. Initially working for a prostitution ring, she agreed to get married in order to obtain French papers. She works for a very demanding French-American couple.

A COLD AND DISTANT WRITING STYLE

Leïla Slimani's style is surprisingly distant and non-judgmental. This is because the writer wishes to tell the story of events as objectively as possible, without passing judgment.

A non-fiction novel?

There is almost a journalistic approach in *Chanson douce*, Leïla Slimani's first profession. This approach is reminiscent of the Anglo-Saxon genre of the *non-fiction novel*, in which the narrative reports real facts while using the techniques of fiction. In this way, despite the initial revelation, the writer introduces a surprising suspense. The use of the present tense gives the story the feel of a clinical account of events. The sentences are short, right from the start of the story. Indeed, the first words are terse: "The baby is dead". This sharp writing is surprising, especially when it states the fate of the two children with an appearance of detachment: "Adam is dead. Mila is going to die".

Writing from a distance

The ending of the novel with direct speech, namely Louise's injunction to the children, 'Children, come. You're going to take a bath", is indicative of the author's desire to keep a distance from the facts and not to dwell on the horror of the double crime. In this respect, it is interesting to note that the last chapter is devoted to the policewoman Nina Dorval, who is in charge of the reconstruction: she is the one who, in a way, will take over the narrative of the crime. The narrative voice moves away out of modesty. This distance is reminiscent of Emmanuel Carrère's cold narrative in his novel *L'Adversaire, which is* also about a crime story.

Understanding rather than judging

There is never any sensationalism in *Chanson douce*. Leïla Slimani never sinks into a pathetic register, despite the horror of the double murder. Moreover, only the useful details for the plot are given. The narrative voice is modest and above all not moralising. The writer does not judge her character. Thus, the use of internal focus allows the story to be limited to Louise's thoughts and feelings rather than reporting them from an external point of view. As Leïla Slimani herself has said: "A writer tries to understand and not to judge".

AVENUES FOR REFLECTION

A FEW QUESTIONS FOR FURTHER REFLECTION...

- Are Myriam and Paul responsible for the drama?

- Can we feel compassion for Louise?

- Why doesn't the story focus more on the children?

- How is this novel similar in some ways to a tragedy?

- Can we apply to Louise the qualification of the tragic hero according to Racine in the preface to Andromache: "neither completely good nor completely evil"?

- Is the novel *Chanson douce* a fictionalized crime story?

- In what way is Leïla Slimani's novel similar to a closed-door film?

- What similarities can be drawn between *Chanson douce* and *L'Adversaire* by Emmanuel Carrère?

- From what point of view can we compare *Chanson douce* and *Les Bonnes* by Jean Genet?

TO GO FURTHER

REFERENCE EDITION

SLIMANI L., *Chanson douce*, Paris, Éditions Gallimard, 2016.

Your opinion is important to us!
Leave a comment on the website of your online bookshop
and share your favourites on social networks!